COPPERHEAD MOON

A Clay Jared Western

R. Annan

Copperhead Moon
Copyright 2015 R. Annan
E. 1.1
WGA Reg. #: R31531 (8/14/15)

Photography © L. Annan

Editor: Karren Tolliver

One Vision Publishing
e-Book ISBN: 978-1-942338-37-6
Print Book ISBN: 978-1-942338-36-9

Western books by R. Annan:

Fight for the Lazy M
The Gunfighter in Winter
Long Ride to Hell's Kitchen
Owl Hawks
Gunfight at Barfield Springs
Shootout at Sanctuary City
Last Days of a Gunfighter
The Red Bandana

Dedicated to:

Fans of the Classical Western Genre

1.

The ranchers in Saggersville, Kansas, met at the Cattlemen's Association the last Friday of every month from six to midnight to shoot the breeze, drink, fart, and tell tall tales. Of course some were there to discuss serious business, too. Among them was Jag Van Buren, the biggest man in the room. He stood heads above the others.

Sixty-year-old Van Buren, owner of the Circle V, had a hawkish nose and protruding, wide chin that gave him a stern look. The sides of his bushy head of hair had long ago turned gray. Although he no longer rode out with the cowboys except on roundups, his hands were still calloused and his face brown from the wind and sun.

Van Buren waited for Arny Beckett, owner of the small Flying B Ranch. While he waited, he drank from his own private stock of Kentucky Bourbon shipped in at his request. As owner of the biggest spread in the valley, he usually got whatever he wanted, either by hook or crook, or any other way.

Arny Beckett, a short, stocky man, came in about seven in the evening and walked slowly up to the bar and ordered a whiskey. He didn't see Van Buren at first and when he did his face took on a sour look.

"Oh, hi, Mr. Van Buren."

"Good evening, Arny," Van Buren said with a big smile. "The drink's on me."

"No thanks," Beckett insisted. "I got it." He dropped an eagle on the bar, waited for his drink, and started to walk away.

Van Buren stepped in front of him, pinning him back against the bar, putting a hand on Beckett's shoulder. The smaller man looked questioningly up at him.

"Can I talk to you, Beckett?" It sounded more like a threat than a request.

"Maybe later. They're waiting for me at the poker table, Mr. Van Buren."

"It'll only take a moment, Arny." This sounded a little friendlier.

Beckett knew there was no way out.

"Alright," he said flatly in a somewhat irritated tone of voice.

"I'm upping my offer to six," Van Buren said quickly. "Six an acre will net you six thousand. And that's more than fair."

"I'm sorry, Mr. Van Buren, but I'm already in negotiations with a buyer for eight an acre." It wasn't true. Beckett said it at the spur of the moment to get Van Buren off his back for good.

"To who? Snell?" Ed Snell was another big rancher in the valley.

"No, not Snell."

"Who, then?"

"A man from St. Louis."

"St. Louis? You sold out to a tenderfoot?"

"The bank in St. Louis is working up the papers," Beckett said. He brushed Van Buren's hand off his shoulder and walked away.

The big rancher stared after Beckett until he was lost in the crowd then turned back to his drink. He tossed it down in one gulp, slammed the empty shot glass down on the bar, and walked out into the night cursing to himself. He didn't like being handled and Arny Beckett had handled him.

Van Buren went from the Cattlemen's Association down the street to the Dirty Boot Saloon. It was Friday night and the place was packed with cowboys and bar girls. Oil lamps hung from the ceiling rafters casting shadows against the walls. No one noticed him, which was what he wanted.

He searched around the room and finally found the man he was looking for. It was Clay Jared, the ramrod he hired two years ago. Jared sat with his sidekick, Frank Dunn, a young cowboy he'd hired along with Jared.

When Jared saw his boss looking down at him, he and Dunn stood up with a surprised look on their faces.

"Can we talk, Clay?" Van Buren said. "Alone?"

Jared nodded to Dunn and the kid took his drink and melted into the shadows. He and Van Buren sat down.

"You want a drink, boss?" Jared asked.

The cowboy was a handsome forty-something with a sort of roguish look. He was well built from working on the range. His face was covered in a short beard that gave him a relaxed look, as if he didn't care about what anyone thought about him. The women liked that, along with his southern twang.

Van Buren refused the offer of a drink.

"What, then?"

Van Buren studied Jared's face for a moment and wondered why he was here, in the Kansas outback. Maybe he was on the run like a lot of his cowboys. Some were deserters from the Civil War. A few had served then deserted on the battlefield. Some robbed banks and trains and were hiding from the law. Others were hiding from the rope. But as long as they did their job, Van Buren looked the other way. It didn't matter to him one way or the other. Only loyalty mattered.

But Jared had the look of a gentleman of the south. One could see he came from a good family. Had he cast it all away? Was he on the run like the others? What was his story? Perhaps someday Van Buren would find out.

"Maybe I will have that drink, Clay," Van Buren said in a fatherly way.

Jared left the table long enough to get another shot glass. It was filthy. Van Buren stared at it as Jared poured him a shot of rotgut from the bottle on the table. Hell, the whiskey would kill the germs. He drank it.

"What's bothering you, boss?" Jared asked.

"I just had a talk with Arny Beckett. He told me he was selling out to some carpetbagger from St. Louis."

"He needs an ass-kicking," Jared said.

"He needs something more permanent, if you get my drift."

Jared nodded. "Yeah. Maybe he does at that."

"I can't have him selling out like that," Van Buren said. He took another sip of the rotgut. "I need the Flying B bad."

"The water?"

"And the graze," the rancher said. "I wish the little shit would just listen. Or maybe disappear."

"What good would that do, if he's already sold the ranch, boss?"

"He ain't signed any papers yet."

"I see," Jared said nodding.

"I want that ranch, Clay," Van Buren said as if in pain. "Have you ever killed a man, son?"

"Yeah. A few."

"Would one more matter?"

"Not to me."

"Have you seen his wife?"

"Yeah."

"Nice, isn't she?"

Jared nodded. "More than nice, boss."

Van Buren paused for a moment and then took the gamble. "Would you do it for two hundred?"

"Do what?" He wanted to make Van Buren say it.

"Kill him?"

There was a heavy silence. The noise around them seemed to close in.

"Hell, boss, I'd do it fer the pleasure of it. I hate the rotten son of a bitch."

"You do?" Van Buren was elated. Was Jared serious or was it the whiskey doing the talking?

"I sure as heck do," the cowboy said. He was a bit glassy-eyed.

"The shitty little runt treated me like a piss ant tonight, Clay," Van Buren said. "I felt like strangling him to death right then and there."

The cowboy nodded. Van Buren continued.

"He's over at the Cattlemen's Association right now, playing cards. At about midnight, he'll go see his whore over at the Pearl Hotel. After that he'll head for home to see his beloved wife and daughter." Van Buren sneered. "A nice Christian man."

Jared chuckled.

"I saw him comin' outta church last week with his wife and daughter," the cowboy said.

"I know. My wife and I were there, too. We see them every week." He paused for a moment. "You sure you don't want that two hundred, son?"

Jared gave that a quick thought. "Ah, no, boss. Not unless I have to go on the run. You never can tell. But I might need some money if something goes wrong."

"Sure. I understand," Van Buren said, smiling like a snake. "Well, I have to go, Clay."

"Sure, boss," the cowboy said. "See ya tomorrow."

Van Buren nodded and left. Frank Dunn came back out of the shadows.

"Did you get that, kid?"

"Most of it. You gonna do it? Kill Arny Beckett?"

"Sure," Jared said. "If anybody needs killin' it's that son of a bitch."

"Why? What's Beckett done ta you?"

Jared took a drink and looked straight ahead as if seeing something in the crowd.

"He's a bad husband."

The young cowboy burst out laughing.

"You're gonna drill him because he's a bad husband?"

"Yep."

"You better lay off the rotgut. It's eatin' away yer brain!" Then after a pause, "Are you serious?"

"Never been more serious in my life."

Suddenly Jared burst out laughing.

"Yer joshin' me, ain't ya?"

"Hell yes, kid!"

"But I jest heard you tell the boss you'd kill Beckett!"

"Did I?"

"You sure as hell did!"

"Hell, he didn't think I was serious. If he did he's dumber than a hoot owl."

"Then yer not gonna kill Arny Beckett?"

"Hell no, kid. Hell no!"

Three hours later Clay Jared was waiting in a stand of pine trees next to the road outside of Saggersville waiting to ambush Arny Beckett.

A copper colored moon was rising in the southwest.

2.

The old coach road out of Saggersville looped east of the Flying B Ranch towards Wichita, sixty miles northeast. Jared tied his horse to a tree and hunkered down to wait.

Over towards the southwest he saw the tip of a brownish red moon above the tops of the pines. It had a strange, dull, coppery color to it and seemed to shimmer in the coolness of the October air. Coyotes howled down the line and night birds flew close to the ground.

Jared pulled the collar of his denim jacket up around his neck to keep out the chill.

As the cowboy waited, his mind drifted and memories from the past came flowing out like the pages of a book being slowly turned by an invisible hand.

Images of his family plantation outside of Richmond, Virginia, and the gay parties and balls roiled up like a groundswell. Memories of dancing, music, and white-gloved Negro servants echoed in his mind. He recalled his first horse and gun, an old 1851 Navy .36 caliber percussion given to him by his Uncle Remmy. It was old Remmy who had taken the time to teach young Clayton Jared, Jr., to ride and shoot. He recalled his sister Jenny's smiling face. His father was but a shadowy bearded figure who beat him for minor infractions of the family code, such as listening to the stories the slaves told around the sorghum vats. A young slave, Vim, was Clay's best friend and showed him how to catch catfish and throw a knife.

When the war started in 1861, Clay Jr. was just fourteen. His two older twin siblings, Larch and Tell, both eighteen, got caught up in the Conscription Act. They were killed at Vicksburg in 1862. When the Adjustment Act of 1864 lowered the age to seventeen, Clay became eligible.

The boy's father was about to march him down to the recruitment center when his mother intervened. They argued for hours over the fate of the young boy. Finally, in the middle of the night, she sent Clay to see Uncle Remmy. The old man packed some food and gave the boy a brand new 1862 Navy, .36 caliber centerfire Colt revolver and had him saddle up to ride out.

"Head west, my boy," old Remmy said. "There'll be others goin' that way. Just follow them. I'll see you after the war, kid," old Remmy said as he slapped Clay's horse on the rump and sent it running.

For three long years young Clay Jared dodged, swerved, and ducked his way west, following a river of men, young and old, evading the law. Among them were men of every kind, cutthroats, gamblers, crooks, and thieves of every sort, the dregs of humanity that preyed on each other as they rolled west. The good didn't survive unless they paid for protection.

Thousands were left dead along the trails. Clay had to fight off attack after attack to keep his horse and gun. He killed a man the first week out. After that it was a natural thing to do. By the time the war was over he was in Abilene. At the age of twenty he had killed more men than he cared to remember.

After a few years in Abilene, he returned home to find his family's plantation burned to the ground, ravaged by the brutality of war. The only thing left was the Jared family plot. The gravestones were overgrown with vines and weeds. Clay Jared's family had ceased to exist. He was the last of the line.

He headed west again.

In the coming years Jared tried his hand at about every job imaginable. He was a security guard on a riverboat and a broncobuster on a ranch. He went on long trail drives and played cards for a living. He fell in and out of love and was shot and wounded numerous times but always managed to live. As could be expected, all this put a hard edge on Clay Jared.

One day he found himself in the town of Saggersville, a wild cow town in the badlands of Kansas, south of Wichita. He was ready to take a break from drifting and went down to the stockyards to check the information board for jobs. That was where he met the kid Frank Dunn, also on the drift. Dunn reminded him of himself when he was young.

They rode out to the Circle V Ranch together and were both hired.

All through this long, aimless journey, Clay carried one special piece of the past with him. It was a pocket watch that old Remmy had given to him. It had Clay's name engraved in it and Clay cherished it because it kept him close to the man he loved more than his father.

As he waited in the pine trees off to the side of the road, Clay took the watch from the pocket of his Levis and checked the time. It was two in the morning. Just as he put it back he heard the sound of a rider in the distance coming from the direction of town. He stepped closer to the road.

The copper colored moon was high in the western sky now, and shadows seemed to creep across the road out of the trees. An owl hooted mournfully somewhere back in the pines.

When Arny Beckett was fifty feet away, Jared stepped out into the middle of the road. The rancher saw him and stopped about thirty feet away and stared, trying to figure out who it was. He finally recognized the cowboy.

"Is thet you, Jared?"

There was no one to see what was going to happen except the copperhead colored moon and the hoot owl.

3.

Some years back, Jim Garrison was the blacksmith in Saggersville. When his wife died, he and his daughter Kate ran the concession along with the town stable. It was a fairly thriving business. Kate was a hard worker but Garrison wanted more for his little girl. Eventually he arranged with rancher Tully Beckett to have his son Arnold court and marry her.

At first Kate refused. She had gone to school with Arny and didn't like him. He had a reputation as a bully and beat up other kids just for looking at him the wrong way. But Kate married Arny Beckett to please her father. He had fought on the Union side in the Civil War, was wounded and in bad health.

Kate's father died a year after she and Arny were married. Beckett's parents died soon after, first his father, and then his mother.

For the first few years the marriage went well, but after their daughter Nona was born, Beckett began acting strange.

He became quarrelsome and short tempered. The ranch, which started out with twelve thousand acres, was reduced to six thousand, half its original size. To keep up with a bank loan, Arny sold cattle piecemeal to nearby ranches at a loss. Instead of two cows per acre they were down to one per acre, a mere six thousand head.

The only advantage to this was that the Flying B cattle had plenty of graze and water, making them the biggest and fattest beeves in the valley.

Arny Beckett, for the most part, was indifferent when it came to finances. He drank and gambled and missed bank payments. Things very quickly got close to the edge for the Beckett ranch.

It was the bank manager, Mort Segal, who suggested they find a buyer. He suggested Jag Van Buren, owner of the Circle V, as a possibility and arranged a meeting of the two at the bank. It didn't go over well. Beckett and Van Buren had a deep dislike for each other. It was more a clash of personalities than anything else. It was putting two different breeds of animals in the same cage. They were opposites in every way. While Van Buren was tall, Beckett was short.

Van Buren was big and powerful, Beckett was little and weak.

Knowing Beckett was in trouble with the bank, Van Buren tried to get Beckett to sell low. To fight this, Beckett spread the rumor around that a rich man from St. Louis was interested in buying the Flying B and was offering top dollar.

He was hoping Van Buren would swallow the bait and offer to buy high.

But Arny Beckett's plans came to an abrupt end when Clay Jared met him on the Saggersville road on the night of the copperhead moon. Three days later, on a Sunday afternoon, he was given a proper burial in the Saggersville Cemetery on the west edge of town. Many people came to the funeral.

Clay Jared and Frank Dunn stood on the porch of the Dirty Boot Saloon staring west at the people as they started down from the cemetery into town.

"Looks like he's been planted," Dunn said.

"Yeah," Jared said. "Let's go pay our respects to the widow."

The two cowboys stepped down into the road and walked briskly up to the church near the cemetery where the buckboards were. Just as they got there, Kate and Nona Beckett walked through the cemetery gate and over to the church. The cowboy intercepted her at the buckboard.

"Mrs. Beckett, ma'am," Jared said. "I'd like to offer you my condolences, if I may."

"Tell your boss Mr. Van Buren that the Flying B is not for sale. Not to him or to anyone else."

Jared removed his hat as Dunn and Nona sized each other up. The brisk cold October wind blew hard against them. The women held onto their bonnets.

"I'm not here on his behalf, Mrs. Beckett," Jared said respectfully. "I'm just here on behalf of the Circle V cowboys to say how sorry we are over Arny's death, ma'am. And I'm especially sorry. He was a good man."

Kate Beckett stared hard at Jared.

"If you think that sir, then I guess you didn't know my husband very well, did you?"

For a moment Jared was caught off-guard.

"Ah, no ma'am, I guess I didn't," Jared admitted.

Kate and Nona climbed up on the buckboard.

"Is that all, Mr. Jared?" Kate asked.

"I just wanted to say if there's anything I can help you with, anything at all, please feel free to call on me. And I say that sincerely, ma'am. Either me or my partner here will come running."

Kate Beckett gave Jared a patronizing stare.

"Why on earth would I ever need your help, sir?" Her voice was as cold as the October wind.

"I'm just sayin', ma'am." Jared suddenly felt stupid and small. "I'm sorry if I offended you. I didn't mean to." He put his hat back on and stepped back as Kate Beckett snapped the reins and started the buckboard moving west.

"Goodbye, Miss Nona," young Dunn yelled. She ignored him.

Jared chuckled. "Kid, I think we both just shot ourselves in the foot."

The cold wind blew down the now empty street of Saggersville. The two cowboys pulled the collars of their coats up around their necks and shivered. They walked bent over back to the Dirty Boot Saloon to get a drink of rotgut.

4.

A week after Arny Beckett's funeral, Van Buren sent for his ramrod.

"You wanted to see me, boss?' Jared stood facing the desk in Van Buren's study. Mrs. Van Buren, a big, hefty woman, gave him a condescending glance and left the room. She and her husband had been arguing but stopped when Clay came in. Van Buren waited until his wife's footsteps faded on the stairs to the second floor. He sat down behind his desk looking agitated.

"Damn woman. Always nagging about something. Now she's complaining about the noise the men make at the bunkhouse on the weekends."

"It's their time to howl, boss," the ramrod said. "They work hard all week."

"I know, I know," the rancher said with a sigh. "Still, maybe you could put up a sign telling them to hold it down with all the yelling and singing and all."

"Sure, boss," Jared said. "Is that all?"

He waited as Van Buren shifted some papers around on his desk.

"No. Sit down, Clay." Jared took a chair near the desk. Van Buren got a cigar from the cigar box and lit it. He blew a cloud of smoke towards Jared.

"She's the problem now. I figured with him gone she'd fold, but she's holding on." He paused a moment to think. "I guess we'll have to do something about her, too."

"Whatta you have in mind, boss?"

"I don't know. What do you suggest?"

Jared pretended to ponder the question. "Well, I don't really know, boss, being as she's a widow and all, and has a daughter. We could maybe wait her out."

Van Buren laughed. "Wait her out? Is that all you can think of? Come on now. You can do better than that, son."

Jared knew the game. He and Van Buren had played it before. The rancher would try to get him to commit himself then he would order the ramrod to do it. If anything went wrong, then Van Buren would blame him. If it was illegal then the rancher would have that on him. Jag Van Buren was a very crafty man with a warped mind.

Jared finally said, "I could go out there and threaten her and her daughter and scare the hell out of them."

"Her men would jump you, wouldn't they?"

"They might if I was all by myself, but I'd take the kid with me. He's fast with a gun."

Van Buren liked that idea. "Yeah. Between the two of you, you could wipe them out and say they braced you first. If the woman got in the way, well, so what? It wasn't your fault."

The rancher sat back in his chair and visualized it all happening. He chuckled then looked serious.

"How's it feel ta murder a man, Jared?" It sounded as if a lawyer had asked it.

Jared shrugged. "Who, me, boss? I never murdered anyone, did I?"

"Sure you did, son," Van Buren said. "You murdered her husband." He smiled. "What if she found out? I bet she'd have you arrested. Go to yer hangin'. She'd hate yer guts, boy. Hate yer guts."

This was how Van Buren always turned, mean and sadistic, taking pleasure in tormenting some low-life cowboy. Jared forced a chuckle to show he wasn't bothered, that he was above it.

"When are you going out there, Jared?"

"To the Flying B? Whenever you want, boss. Just say the word."

"Do it tomorrow evening when all her cowhands are back from the range."

"Sure. Whatever you say, boss."

"Kill as many as you can. Hell, if she gits in the way, well, accidents do happen, don't they?"

"They sure do, boss, they sure do." Jared chuckled, wondering if this man thought he was stupid.

Van Buren was talking like a fool. Did he want the Flying B Ranch so bad that he would have Jared kill the woman and her daughter? Did he think the cowboy would do such a thing? At that moment Jared felt like drawing his gun and shooting the rancher dead.

"Is that all, boss?" the ramrod asked.

"Yeah. You kin get back to work now," Van Buren said as if dismissing a servant.

On the way down to the bunkhouse, Jared reached for his pocket watch and found he didn't have it on him. At first he thought he might have lost it that night in the pine stand but remembered he had just looked at it yesterday.

When he got to the bunkhouse he looked under his pillow. Sometimes he put it there so he could see what time it was when he awoke in the morning. It wasn't there.

He looked under his bunk and finally in his saddlebag. Dunn noticed and came up to him.

"What's wrong, you lost yer bill fold?"

"My watch."

"Hell, you kin buy another one in town."

"This one is special," Jared said. "Very special."

"Oh."

Jared had a bad feeling about that watch.

5.

Clay Jared and young Frank Dunn rode across Circle V land onto the Flying B. It was midday and the early October sun was already heading down the western sky. The wind picked up and sent clusters of gray tumbleweed rolling across the surrounding fields.

They rode through the yard gate and stopped to look around. Hearing a noise behind the ranch house, they dismounted and walked around to the corral. A dozen quarter horses stood watching as Kate Beckett, wearing a dress, was trying to plant a new fence post. The old one was rotted at the bottom and lay on the ground a few feet away.

She wasn't doing very well. The dress kept getting in her way.

"The hole ain't deep enough, ma'am," Jared said.

He grabbed the fence post and pulled it up out of the hole inside the rails. Frank Dunn grabbed the nearby shovel and began digging out more dirt. The ground was solid from the cold. It took a while but he dug out another ten inches of soil and Jared dropped the post in behind the two rails. Dunn packed in the dirt. Jared looked around for the hammer and nails. He spotted them and drove a spike through each rail into the post.

"Thank you, Mr. Jared," Kate said. "You make it look easy. You, too, Mr. Dunn." She wiped dirt from her hands.

"My pleasure, ma'am," the young cowboy said.

"What brings you two this far from the Circle V, Mr. Jared?"

A cold wind came in from the nearby field and nipped at their faces.

"Well, ma'am, we were out ridin' when we thought we smelt coffee brewin' over on the Flyin' B. Naturally we had to investigate."

"Of course," Kate chuckled, brushing hair out of her eyes.

"Where's yer handy man, Mrs. Beckett?" Jared asked.

"Can't afford one. Come on up to the house." Kate said, as she walked away, pulling up the collar of her jacket.

Before the cowboy could reply, she led the way over, wondering what his interest in her was. For a tough ramrod he seemed to have a tender respect for women.

Nona was in the kitchen by the stove. She was wearing an apron. Young Dunn's eyes caught fire and danced at the sight of her. She knew he was smitten and enjoyed it.

"Before you say it, I'm still not selling, Mr. Jared."

Jared chuckled. "Then let's talk about somethin' else, ma'am. Anything you want."

"Please sit," Kate said as she went to the sideboard and started preparing the coffee.

Jared watched her work. There was something about her that reminded him of his mother, the way she stood, her back firm. She was a strong woman of the west. She knew he was studying her and smiled, her face turned away so he couldn't see. Finally, she had the coffee pot on the hot, cast-iron stove.

"Where are you from, Mr. Jared?" Kate asked. "All you cowboys are from somewhere."

"Virginia."

"Oh? Did you fight in the war?"

"No, ma'am. When they started taking seventeen-year-olds I ran off."

"You deserted?"

"My mother lost two sons. I was the last one."

Kate nodded. "I see. I would have done the same thing, I'm sure."

Nona turned to young Frank Dunn.

"What about you, Mr. Dunn? Where are you from?"

"Chicago, ma'am," Dunn said, blushing a bit.

"Chicago?" It was as if Nona didn't believe him or Chicago was on the moon. "Why did you come way out here?"

"I read about Kansas in the magazines. About the wild west and all."

Nona giggled. "And you believed it? You're dumber than you look."

"Nona Beckett!" Kate said. "You apologize to Mr. Dunn. Right now!"

"It's okay, ma'am," Dunn chuckled. "I've been called worse things than a dumb cowboy!"

"Well, it's true, momma. He's a tenderfoot. I bet he can't even throw a lariat or bust a bronc. One day he'll probably shoot himself in the foot."

Jared burst out laughing.

Young Dunn smiled. "Is that what you think, Miss Nona?"

"Yep. That's what I think, Frank Dunn," Nona Beckett said. "I don't even know why you carry a gun. Somebody will surely brace and kill you."

"You got a can?"

"What?" Nona Beckett was suddenly startled.

"You got a can?" Dunn repeated.

"What for?"

"I'd like to show you what a bad shot I am."

Nona turned to her mother. "Momma, do we still have one of them empty peach cans around?"

Kate reached down near the stove into a pine box and shifted some things around. She finally found an empty peach can. She handed it to her daughter. Nona handed it to Dunn.

"Here's yer old peach can, Mr. Dunn," Nona said in a haughty voice. "Whatta ya gonna do with it? Use it fer a spittoon?"

"No, ma'am," the young cowboy said as he stood up. "If you'll please come outside with me, I'll show you."

"After you, sir," Nona said.

They all went outside. A stiff wind was blowing across the yard, snapping at the women's hair and dresses. The young cowboy moved a few steps away from the others and tossed the can upwards. The wind caught it and it rose spinning in the air.

Frank Dunn's right hand became a blur as he drew. His left hand came across the hammer of his Colt and he fanned off three quick shots. The peach can jerked upward and zigzagged from side to side. Then the young cowboy put three more holes in it before it hit the ground. He quickly reloaded the Colt.

"Oh my God! Did you see thet, momma?"

Kate Beckett nodded. "I did. I surely did."

Nona ran across the yard, picked up the can, and brought it back.

"I'm gonna keep this," she said. "It'll make a darn good waterin' can."

They all laughed and followed Nona back into the house.

"Who taught you to shoot like that, Mr. Dunn?" Kate asked over a cup of coffee and piece of peach pie.

"My father was a gunsmith. He sold guns and rifles."

"I see. You are very good."

The remark embarrassed the young cowboy and he started blushing again. Nona saw it and laughed. "He's sorta cute when he blushes, momma." They all chuckled, including Dunn.

"How many cowhands do you have, Mrs. Beckett?" Jared asked.

"Now? Only five. They're out on the range. After Arnold died a bunch of them left. I couldn't pay them anyway, so it's just as well."

Jared nodded. "I see."

"I feel like selling, Mr. Jared," Kate said, "but my dislike for Mr. Van Buren always stops me. That and my pride. I'm not a quitter. I like the Flying B and I'll hang on to it as long as I can. If they want it, they'll have to take it away from me."

Jared smiled sympathetically.

Kate went on. "I've put a lot of hard work and sweat into this place and I'm not going to walk away without a fight."

"Do you have a ramrod, ma'am?"

"No. Why do you ask?"

"The fall count and brand season is about over. You don't have enough men to pull in your cattle and brand calves. You're way behind schedule."

Kate laughed. "Right now the Flying B isn't flying very well, is it, Mr. Jared?"

"What about the bank, ma'am?" Dunn asked.

"Well, that's another matter. I'll most likely have to sell if they decide it's time to foreclose. I can't see any way out. This is your real west, Mr. Dunn, not the storybook kind."

Dunn nodded and said no more.

After a while the two cowboys thanked their host and got up to leave. Jared looked around. The kitchen was warm and friendly. He hated to leave.

"You can tell your Mr. Van Buren it won't be long before he owns the Flying B, Mr. Jared."

Jared turned to look at Kate Beckett and smiled.

"If I were to bet on that ma'am, I'd put all my money on you."

"Would you, really, Mr. Jared?"

"Oh, yes, ma'am. I surely would."

On the way back to the Circle V the two cowboys talked.

"You acted like you cared about her, boss," Dunn said.

"Did I?"

"Yep. The way you kept looking at her. Nona saw it too."

Jared only shrugged and kept going. The wind started howling behind them. The ramrod felt conflicted. Kate Beckett needed his help but he was working for Van Buren.

He was in a bad position and he didn't like it.

6.

"Well," Van Buren asked, "did you go out there and threaten her like you said you would?"

"Sure, boss." Clay answered.

"What happened?"

"Nothing."

"Nothing?" Van Buren sounded disappointed. "How come?"

"She's down to five old, broken down cowhands and the bank is about to foreclose. Hell, boss, she'll be finished in a few months."

"A few months? I can't wait a few months, Jared!"

"Why not?"

"Because I don't want to!" Van Buren yelled. "You keep promising to deliver the Flying B and you don't. All you do is talk."

"Alright," Jared said. "Give me one more week. I'll get it done."

The big rancher simmered down a bit. He sighed and jabbed a finger in Jared's face, nodding. "Okay. You got one more week. If you don't get it done I'll make my own move on her. And it won't be pretty."

"Sure, boss. I'll do it."

After Jared left, Van Buren sat in his study mulling over his situation. He was beginning to think Jared was purposely stalling him. Maybe the Beckett woman had gotten to him. She wasn't bad looking and she was smart. Maybe she had worked on Jared and turned his head. Maybe it was time to cut the ramrod loose, get rid of him.

That wouldn't be easy to do. Jared had a lot of dirt on the rancher. It was Van Buren who asked Jared to kill Arny Beckett, so the cowboy had that on him. But who would believe a cowboy's word against his?

Jag Van Buren pondered the problem of getting rid of the ramrod. He considered having him killed. There were men among his cowboys who would do it for a price, men like Bart Gowdy who he knew had a purple past and was laying low. He'd been watching Gowdy for a long time now. Perhaps it was time to use him.

It wouldn't be too difficult. All he had to do was threaten to expose Gowdy to the law. Not that he ever would, but it could give the rancher the leverage he needed to control the old outlaw. And he'd heard rumors that Gowdy didn't like Jared.

A day after Jared and Dunn had gone out to the Flying B Ranch, Marshal Talbot and his two deputies came from Saggersville to see him.

"Howdy, Mr. Van Buren," the marshal said.

"What brings you to the Circle V, marshal?"

"I'd like ta talk to yer ramrod Jared, sir."

"He's out with the boys on the north sector right now, marshal. He won't be back until evening," Van Buren explained, lying. He wasn't sure where his ramrod was but hoped he was dealing death to the Flying B cowboys.

The marshal stroked his chin and nodded.

"I see. Well, tell him ta come see me in town when he gets back."

"Sure," Van Buren said.

Marshal Talbot and his deputies left. That evening the rancher cornered Jared.

"Where you been, Jared?"

"Scaring off the last of her cowboys." It wasn't true. Dunn and him were looking for Flying B lost cattle.

Van Buren chucked. "Good work."

"Thanks, boss."

"Oh, the marshal was out here. He wanted ta see you about somethin'. Better go see him."

"Now?"

"Yeah. It sounded urgent. Best get it out of the way tonight."

"Sure, if you say so."

The ramrod went down to the bunkhouse to talk to Dunn.

"You want me ta go with you?"

"No. No need to."

Jared rode into town and found the marshal at his desk waiting. His two deputies were with him.

"You wanted to see me, marshal?"

"Yep," the marshal said.

"What about?"

"I think you damn well know, Jared!"

The marshal opened a drawer in his desk and pulled out Jared's pocket watch. He held it up by its chain.

"How did you get hold of that, marshal?"

"It was found out on the road at the spot where Arny Beckett was murdered."

Jared's brain scrambled for an explanation.

"Well, it must have been planted there because I had it right up until a few days ago when it came up missing."

The marshal chuckled. "Sure, it did."

As Jared reached for the watch the two deputies grabbed him by the arms.

"I'm not lying, marshal," Jared insisted.

"I'll tell you what, son," the lawman said. "If the coroner's inquiry clears you, I'll give it back."

"Coroner's inquiry? What the hell's that?" Jared asked.

"It's where you sit and watch while the medical examiner from the county determines if it's likely that Arny

Beckett's death was deliberate," Marshal Talbot said. He chuckled. "Thet's all it is, friend."

"Hell, marshal, everybody knows somebody shot him!"

"Sure, but we gotta point the finger at the shooter, don't we?"

"And I guess it looks like me," the ramrod said solemnly.

The marshal chuckled again. "It sure does."

"Can I ask who found the watch?"

"Sure. A cowboy named Nobby Brown."

"Nobby Brown!" Jared acted surprised.

"That's right."

Suddenly the cowboy realized he was being framed. He wondered if Van Buren was involved.

"I'll have ta lock you up till after the trial, cowboy," the marshal said. "After that you'll either walk or hang. Better get a lawyer, my friend."

"Hell, I don't know any lawyers, marshal."

The marshal looked at Jared. His face softened.

"Alright, son, I'll see what I kin do. There's a new kid here in town from California. Just out of law school. Maybe he's dumb enough ta work fer ya"

They locked Jared in the only cell the jailhouse had. It was empty. He sat there on the cot thinking about the lawyer mentioned by the marshal. He sure couldn't be too smart.

A smart lawyer wouldn't come to an outback cattle town like Saggersville unless he was desperate.

7.

Bart Gowdy, Cord McBride, Windy Johnson and Nobby Brown were rustlers. Some years ago they operated in the Brownsville area of Texas running stolen cattle into Matamoros, Mexico.

When the Texas Ranger took an interest in Gowdy and his little gang, things got too hot so they headed north to San Antonio and switched to robbing banks. They soon had to ride on again to avoid the law, outrunning posse after posse until they escaped across the Red River into Oklahoma Territory.

They always wore masks so the wanted posters didn't have much to show except their general descriptions.

When Gowdy got seriously wounded and almost died, they decided to look for a place to lay low. They headed north into Kansas and found it to be friendlier. It was there they hired on, with no questions asked, at the Circle V Ranch. They easily blended in with the rest of the hands and laid low while waiting for some opportunity to show itself.

That was five years ago, and during that time Gowdy and his pals saw three ramrods come and go at the Circle V. And now the latest one, smart-assed Clay Jared, was in jail, thanks to quick thinking by Nobby Brown.

It was Brown who laid out the plan to steal Jared's pocket watch and drop it on the road at the exact spot where Arny Beckett was murdered. As Brown was an accomplished pickpocket it wasn't hard to do.

The next step was for Gowdy to talk to Van Buren. And he did. He was soon standing before the rancher's desk in his study. Van Buren looked at the grizzly little man.

Short and stocky, Gowdy had a face covered with stubble. A long red scar ran down the left side of his face, from the forehead to the lower part of his cheek. Gowdy had a small, puckered up mouth. His nose had been flattened in a bar fight in Abilene and pointed sideways on his face. He was just plain ugly and mean looking and Van Buren liked that.

"Who the hell are you?" Van Buren asked with a chuckle. Then he remembered. "Oh, yer Gowdy, ain't you?"

"Yes, sir," Gowdy said, acting very humble.

"You've been with the Circle V about five years now, haven't you?"

"That's right, boss."

Van Buren looked the scurvy little man over again and chuckled.

"Christ! When's the last time you took a bath, Gowdy?" The outlaw chuckled and let the remark fly by. "Well, what the hell do you want? Make it quick. I'm a busy man."

"I see you need a new ramrod, boss, sir."

"What about it?"

"I'd like a shot at the job, sir."

"Oh, you would, huh?"

"Thet little problem you have with the Flying B, sir? I can take thet offin yer hands real pronto."

"How could you do that, Gowdy?"

"My, ah, specialty is movin' cattle, if you git my drift, boss?"

Suddenly Van Buren was interested.

"Do you mean what I think you mean, Gowdy?"

"I know how ta move cattle at night without bein' seen. Make them invisible, so ta speak."

"I see."

"An' I know all about the Flyin' B, how much cattle they got, an' how many cowhands. Thet kind of stuff."

"Go on."

"I'd make it so she'd wake up some mornin' an' find out she's got a lot less cattle than she thought she had."

"What about her cowhands?"

"Some could disappear right along with the cattle."

"And you could do all that?"

"Yes sir, I could. In fact I have. Many times." Gowdy chuckled.

The rancher studied the little man again, looking him carefully up and down.

"Tell me all about yourself, Mr. Gowdy," Van Buren said. "And if you lie to me you will be looking for a job elsewhere, my friend. Do you understand?"

Gowdy told it all. Every bit of it. Van Buren listened, enjoying every incriminating word.

"Very interesting, Mr. Gowdy," the rancher said when the old outlaw was finished revealing his past. He now had enough evidence on Gowdy to have him hung from the highest tree.

Van Buren took two cigars from the cigar box and handed one to Gowdy.

"Do you smoke cigars Mr. Gowdy?"

"When I kin, boss," Gowdy said.

They lit up and blew smoke.

"I'll let the men know you're the new ramrod on the Circle V, Mr. Gowdy."

"Thank you, sir."

The rancher chuckled, thinking Gowdy would have made a good pirate.

"One thing, Gowdy," Van Buren said. "About the Flying B? Don't show any mercy to the women out there. They're all bitches and deserve what's coming to them."

"Just so you know, boss, I don't work alone. I have three pals who hired on here with me. We'd all expect about sixty a month from now on, if ya don't mind?"

Van Buren gave that some consideration for a few moments and nodded.

"Alright. Sixty a month. For the four of you. No one else is to know."

"You got it, boss."

After Gowdy left, Van Buren began to take stock of his situation. If something went wrong he could always say he had no idea what Gowdy was up to. He didn't know he was a notorious rustler and bank robber. How could he? He was just a hardworking, honest rancher, that's all.

Van Buren sat back in his chair and blew a cloud of smoke towards the ceiling, smiling broadly. He was in full control now, and that was the way he liked it.

Jared would soon be dancing on the end of a rope.

8.

Clay Jared was asleep on his cot in the Saggersville jail when the marshal woke him up.

"You've got a visitor, son."

Jared sat up and rubbed the sleep from his eyes. He stretched as the marshal unlocked the door to admit a young man in an expensive looking blue suit into the cell then locked the door again.

"I'm Otis Newman, Mr. Jared," the young man said. He and Jared shook hands.

Jared saw a tall, thin, pale man with rippling black hair combed back on his head. Newman looked about twenty years old and had the ambience of a bookworm, frail and delicate. He had a sincere, good-looking face untouched by wind and sun, which meant he only recently arrived in the west.

"I'm your lawyer, Mr. Jared," the young man said.

"I didn't hire a lawyer, Mr. Newman."

"I'm doing this pro bono. So the town can see what I do. You're my first case."

"Lucky me."

Newman ignored the remark.

"Circuit Judge Thaddeous Morgan will be here in Saggersville in a week," the young lawyer said. "He presides on serious cases such as murder." Jared shrugged. "We'll plead not guilty."

"I did it."

"Then we'll plead insanity."

"I'm not crazy."

"You were drunk, perhaps?"

"I had a few but I wasn't drunk."

The young man thought about that for a moment.

"Well, I guess that simplifies things somewhat. We'll plead guilty and ask for mercy."

Jared yawned and nodded. "Sure. Whatever you say, Mr. Newman. Now I'd like to finish my nap, if you don't mind."

"Ah, we should go over the details, shouldn't we?"

"Come back tomorrow, sonny," Jared said. "We'll do it then."

The young man looked dejected. He sighed, nodded, called to the marshal, and quickly left. Jared didn't feel tired any more so he played checkers with the marshal. An hour later Kate Beckett walked into the jailhouse. The marshal searched her for a weapon.

"I'm not here to slip the prisoner a file or gun, marshal."

"I was thinkin' more in the way of you shootin' him, ma'am," the marshal said.

Kate Beckett left that unanswered and walked over to the cell bars and stared in at Jared. He stood up and faced her.

"Is it true?" Jared didn't answer. "They'll hang you, you know." Jared shrugged. "The Judge is Thaddeus Morgan. They call him the hanging judge."

Jared chuckled. "That's good to know, ma'am. I feel better already." He stared into her eyes. "Why did you come?"

She didn't answer but turned to the lawman. "Marshal, I want to report a loss of cattle. It seems there are rustlers in the valley now. And my men are missing."

"All of them?"

"Yes."

"You're out there all alone, ma'am?"

"My daughter and I, yes."

At that moment Frank Dunn came in. A deputy took his gun and put it in the marshal's desk.

"Mrs. Beckett," the young cowboy said removing his hat.

"Frank," Jared said. "You need to go with Mrs. Beckett and stay out at her place."

"Sure. How come?"

"She'll explain that later."

"That's very kind of you, Mr. Jared, but I can't pay Mr. Dunn."

"It doesn't matter. He just quit the Circle V and he needs a place to bunk. Right, kid?"

"Whatever you say, boss."

"I'm not your boss anymore. I'm your pard."

Dunn chuckled. "We ain't married, are we?"

Everyone laughed to break the tension.

"I'll send a deputy out first thing in the morning ma'am," the marshal said. "He'll take a look around."

Dunn went over close to the jail cell.

"Van Buren made Gowdy ramrod. Remember him?"

"Yeah. He's the one always slinkin' around. Has a face like a wet weasel. Hangs out with McBride, Johnson and Brown."

"That's him boss," Dunn said. "The four of them sneak out at night from time ta time and come back near sunrise."

The marshal cut in. "And now Mrs. Beckett is losin' cattle and her men are missing." He stroked his chin. "Now, ain't that a coincidence?"

"Sure is," one of the deputies remarked.

"Maybe I'll take a ride out there myself," the marshal said.

There didn't seem to be anything more to say.

"I'll be leaving," Kate Beckett said. She looked at Jared. "Good luck Mr. Jared."

Frank Dunn got his Colt and went with her. The marshal went over to Jared.

"That's funny, ain't it?"

"What?" Jared asked.

"You kill her husband and she wishes you good luck at the trial. I don't get it."

"Maybe after the trial you will marshal," Jared said.

He went back to finishing his nap.

9.

Judge Thaddeus Morgan looked like a prophet straight out of the Old Testament. Most of his face was hidden behind a bushy gray beard, including his mouth, which was invisible unless he opened it to speak. He had a prominent nose that stuck out between two fiery eyes under a large protruding forehead. These notable features were balanced by two overly large ears that could hear a frog fart from forty feet away.

He looked every bit the hanging judge he was said to be.

The trial was just about to start. The Dirty Boot Saloon was marked off into three sections with tables stacked against the west wall to make room for the proceedings.

Chairs were aligned along the east wall for the six-man jury. The judge's table was near the north wall facing the table and chair for the accused that were a few feet in front of it. There was a testimony chair to the right of the judge's table and about twenty chairs behind the defense's table, near the bat wing doors, for spectators. They were already full.

Outside, the porch was packed and people looked in through the windows. Clay Jared sat in the chair for the accused and the young lawyer, Otis Newman, stood at the table next to him looking at his notes.

There were three cracking sounds as Judge Morgan sounded the gavel to open the trial. The room fell quiet. The Judge stared at Clay Jared. The cowboy stood up.

"Are you Clay Jared, the accused?"

"Yes, Judge."

The Judge shifted his gaze to the young lawyer.

"Are you his lawyer?"

"Otis Newman. Yes, Your Honor, I am Mr. Jared's lawyer." It sounded a little like he was bragging about it. A few people in the crowd chuckled.

"Good," the Judge said. He glanced at Marshal Talbot and nodded in recognition, then cleared his throat. "Now here's how I do things. It's real simple. I ask questions whenever I feel like it." He pointed the gavel at Jared. "You keep yer trap shut unless yer told ta open it. Is thet clear and understood?" Jared nodded. "Alright then," the Judge said.

He paused for a moment to look around the room.

"Mr. Newman, Mr. Jared is accused of murdering a man called, let me see here, oh, yeah, Arnold Beckett. Is thet what he's charged with?"

"Yes. That is so, Your Honor."

"How does he plead?"

"Not guilty."

The old Judge chuckled. "Well, I have your client's statement here, submitted by the marshal, admitting to shooting Mr. Beckett. It says and I quote, 'I shot and killed Arnold Beckett.' It says where and when. Thet sure looks like a murder confession ta me, sonny."

"It doesn't say my client murdered Mr. Beckett, Your Honor. It merely states he killed him."

For a moment the Judge glared at Otis Newman.

"Are you tryin' to be a smart ass, mister?"

"Newman, Your Honor, sir," The young lawyer said.

For a second it looked like the Judge was going to explode on Newman, but he coughed and held it in.

He held up a sheet of paper.

"It says here, in this deposition, thet Mr. Jared met Mr. Beckett one night on the road outside of town an' shot him down in cold blood. As I see it, thet's murder. How do you see it, Mr. Newman?"

"It's not a question of how I see it, Your Honor, it's a question of how the jury sees it when the trial is finished. All Mr. Jared wants is his day in court."

The Judge was taken aback for a moment.

"Oh, he'll get it," the Judge snarled. "Don't you worry about thet." He leaned back in his chair and folded his arms. "Go ahead, sonny. Let's hear yer case. I'll just sit here an' take a nap, if thet's alright with you."

The crowd of spectators laughed and a few jurors chuckled. Otis Newman looked uncertain. This was his first trial and his mind raced in circles trying to decide where to begin.

"Well," the old Judge said sarcastically. "You got any testimony fer the defense of Mr. Jared or is this trial over? He's a sittin' here a waitin'. He kin probably already feel the rope around his neck gettin' tighter and tighter. Soon his eyes will be poppin' out! Haw!"

The crowd liked the Judge's sarcasm and laughed. The young lawyer, it seemed, was in for a beating.

"You kin sit down, Mr. Jared," the Judge said.

Otis Newman looked around at the crowd as if searching for something. Suddenly he stopped and pointed.

"Miss Nona Beckett! Would you please be so kind as to take the testimony chair?"

The entire room went silent. Nona Beckett and her mother sat in the back of the room in the crowd. She looked at her mother. Kate nodded and Nona slowly walked up to the chair by the Judge's table. There was a Bible on the edge of his desk.

"Put yer hand on the Bible and swear to tell the truth," Judge Morgan said in a kindly voice usually not his style. The girl took the oath and sat in the chair.

The young lawyer approached her and cleared his throat.

"Miss Beckett, did you love your father?"

The question sent a murmur through the crowd.

"No. I did not." The answer was even more unexpected.

"Why not?"

"Because he beat me and my mother."

The crowd moaned.

Suddenly the Judge yelled, "You're excused, Miss Beckett. Go back to yer mom."

Nona Beckett got up but kept talking as she walked away.

"He beat my mother when he was drunk and when he was sober! He was not a good father or husband!" she sobbed as she sat down next to her mother.

"What's wrong, Judge?" the young lawyer asked.

"If you don't know, sonny, yer dumber than I figured ya was. Her testimony ain't got nothin' ta do with the charge, thet's what's wrong. Even a jackass with half a brain would know thet!"

Otis Newman looked defeated. Jared stared at him and the young lawyer leaned over. The cowboy whispered something to him.

Newman nodded and addressed the crowd. "Is Doctor Sawyer here?" A short bald headed man in a worn suit standing by the door raised his hand.

"Would you be so kind as to take the testimony chair, Doctor?"

The doctor nodded and walked past the crowd. He took the oath at the Judge's desk and sat down. Judge Morgan leered at Otis Newman.

"This better be relevant, sonny boy."

"Yes, Your Honor," Newman said. He spoke from beside his table, fifteen feet away from the doctor. "Doctor Sawyer, sir, you examined the body of the deceased, Arnold Beckett, did you not?"

"I did," the doctor said.

"What did you find?"

"What do you mean, what did I find?"

"Where was Mr. Beckett shot and from what distance?"

"He was shot once in the heart. As for distance, I would say from about thirty feet away."

"Was whoever shot him facing him?"

"I'd say yes. The bullet came from the front, yes."

"Just one shot?"

"Yes. Just one clean shot."

"And did Mr. Jared visit you with a slight gunshot wound?"

"Yes, he did."

"When?"

"The same night Mr. Beckett was shot."

"Thank you, Doctor Sawyer. That is all," the young lawyer said. Then, before the judge could say a word, Newman called out, "Marshal Talbot, would you please take the testimony chair, sir?"

"Sure," the marshal said.

"This is highly irregular, Mr. Newman," the Judge said. "Is it necessary or are you just fishin' around?"

"I feel it is necessary, Your Honor."

"Hell, I don't mind, Judge. Maybe he'll want to call the Governor next," Marshal Talbot chuckled. The crowd laughed once more. The marshal took the oath and sat in the testimony chair trying not to smile. The young lawyer collected his thoughts.

"Now, marshal, did you find that Mr. Beckett had been robbed?"

"He was not robbed."

"Did you find his gun?"

"We did."

"Was it fired?"

"Yes. Twice."

"Why did you decide to arrest Mr. Jared for the death of Mr. Beckett?"

"Because Mr. Brown, who was coming into town from the Circle V Ranch, came in with a pocket watch. He said he'd found it on the side of the road as he was comin' into Saggersville. It had Mr. Jared's name engraved inside the cover. He showed me where he found it. It was the place where Mr. Beckett's body was discovered."

"When was this?

"Two days after Mr. Beckett was killed."

"I see. And you didn't notice it before?"

"No. That's why I asked Mr. Jared about it."

"What did Mr. Jared say, marshal?"

"He said he'd lost it."

"You didn't believe him?"

"Would you?" the marshal shot back. The crowd chuckled.

"Couldn't someone have stolen the watch from Mr. Jared and placed it there for someone to find?"

"Most people would have kept it instead of turning it in, wouldn't they, Counselor? It was Mr. Jared's bad luck that an honest man found it."

"So, when you confronted Mr. Jared with the watch he confessed? Just like that?"

"Yep. He sang like a canary," the marshal said.

The crowd chuckled again. Otis Newman smiled. The marshal had handled him pretty good.

"Thank you, marshal, no further questions."

Marshal Talbot got up. He walked slowly over to his station, ten feet behind Jared's chair where a deputy with a shotgun stood watching the cowboy.

"Well, is thet all, sonny?" Judge Morgan asked.

"No, Your Honor, I have one last witness, if I may?"

"An' who might that be? The President?" This set the crowd to roaring.

"No, Your Honor."

"Okay then, who?"

"Clay Jared, Your Honor."

The judge nodded.

"Alright, if Mr. Jared wants ta hang himself, go right ahead. Git him up here. I'd like ta see if he kin squirm his way outta this bear trap. It might be fun ta watch."

Otis Newman waited until the crowd settled down, and then said, "Clay Jared, please take the testimony chair."

Jared got up and took the oath.

The room went quiet again as it did from time to time. The crowd stared at the Judge as he leered at Clay Jared, his eyes blazing like two red, hot, burning coals.

"I been a watchin' you, Mr. Jared," the Judge growled. "You been a sittin' there lookin' smug like ya think it's a game a checkers or somethin', pretendin' you ain't scared. But yer scared, alright. I kin see it. You ain't a foolin' me none. Yer ready ta crap yer pants and thet's fer sure. Yer thinkin' about thet hangman's rope, aincha?"

Everyone in the room was fascinated, waiting for Jared to show some sign of fear or some other human emotion. But the cowboy didn't. He sat looking calmly across the room at Kate and Nona Beckett.

"Mrs. Beckett, ma'am," the cowboy said so she could hear. "You might want to take Nona and leave now."

"No, Mr. Jared," Kate said loudly. "We'll stay."

"Then, please forgive me for what I'll be sayin' here this day. I don't mean it to hurt you or Nona."

"That's enough outta you, Jared!" the Judge yelled. "You're here ta answer questions, not ta make a speech! This ain't so side show!"

The crowd didn't seem to like this and showed their discontent with a loud grumble. They had grown weary with the old Judge's displays of sadistic authority. He was going too far. Jared was the underdog and they could easily identify with him.

"And as fer the rest a you, if you don't cut yer yappin' I'll have yer asses thrown out on the street!"

That was not the right thing to say to the inhabitants of Saggersville. It didn't go over well but the Judge failed to see the signs of their displeasure.

"Well, come on, Counselor, get it ta movin'. We ain't got all day here. My bowels is getting' all in an uproar!"

The Judge waited for a laugh but got only a cold stare from the crowd. The young lawyer looked over at Clay Jared and smiled.

"Mr. Jared, we all have a rough picture of what happened that fateful night outside of town but what we don't know is what your motive was. Why did you go after Mr. Beckett? What was the problem between you two? Can you tell us?"

"Sure."

"And start from the beginning, if you would, please, sir?"

Jared cleared his throat. "I'd met Arny Beckett a few times in town. At night he'd come over from the Cattlemen's Association meetings and have a few drinks at the Dirty Boot Saloon. He had a girlfriend over there."

The Judge suddenly cut Jared off.

"Irrelevant! The jury will disregard thet statement!"

"It goes to character, Your Honor," Newman insisted.

"I don't care what it goes to. It's not relevant!"

The young lawyer shrugged.

"What was your relationship with Mrs. Beckett?"

"I met her a few times in town at the mercantile and other places."

"What did you notice about her?"

"Her face was bruised. Her husband had beat her."

"Not relevant!" the Judge yelled once more. "You'd best go back ta law school, sonny!"

"Tell us what really happened on the road that night."

"We know what happened on the road thet night!" the Judge yelled. "He murdered Beckett is what happened!"

"Tell us, in detail, how you killed Mr. Beckett." Otis Newman said, ignoring the Judge. He was determined to get it out. And the crowd wanted to hear every word.

"As Beckett came up the road, I walked out and stood there. When he saw me he stopped."

"What time was it?"

"Two in the morning."

"What happened after he stopped?"

"He asked me what I wanted and I told him I wanted to brace him." Jared said. "He asked me why I wanted to brace him and I said because he cheated on his wife and beat her. Then he said it was nobody's business how he treated his wife. I said it had to be somebody's business because it wasn't right to beat a woman. It was against the code."

Jared paused.

"What did Beckett say to that?"

"He laughed and said I was stupid, that it was a fool's code and he didn't live by no fool's code."

"He said that?"

"Yes."

"What happened next?"

"Well, he said he wasn't going to draw on me unless I gave him cause to draw."

"And you gave him cause?"

"Yes, I did."

"How?"

"I said something about his wife and daughter."

"What did you say?"

Jared looked down at the floor.

"I told him his wife and daughter were whores."

The crowd made a low moaning sound as if wounded.

"What did he do, then?"

"Nothing. He just laughed and said maybe I was right. He still wasn't going to draw on me. Even a coward would have pulled on me for what I said."

"Then what did you do?"

"I told him he could have first shot."

"First shot?"

"Yes. I said he could have first shot."

"Wasn't that dangerous?"

Jared only shrugged and looked at the crowd.

"What happened next?"

"Beckett got down on the road. I waited. He drew and shot at me."

"And he missed?"

"No. He hit me here, in the left side."

And then you shot at him."

"No, just as I drew, he fired off a second shot and hit me high on my left shoulder. Both shots had nicked me good but they weren't serious."

"Then you shot him?"

"Yes. I shot him once in the heart."

Even the old Judge listened quietly. The wind seemed to have gone out of his sails. He sighed deeply and nodded.

"Can you show the jury where Mr. Beckett shot you?"

Jared stood up and removed his shirt. There was a red scar on his left hip and left shoulder.

Jared put his shirt back on and sat down.

"No further questions, Mr. Jared," the lawyer said.

It took the jury of six people ten minutes to return a verdict of self-defense. Young lawyer Otis Newman had tried and won his first case. He shook a hundred hands, passed out his cards, and walked out of the Dirty Boot Saloon smiling with Clay Jared at his side.

10.

The afternoon that Clay Jared got out of jail, he rode out to the Flying B Ranch. The place was deserted except for a buckboard in the yard by the ranch house. As he rode through the gate Kate Beckett came out on the porch carrying a shotgun. Jared stayed in the saddle and raised his hands.

"Don't shoot, ma'am," he chuckled. "I surrender."

Kate laughed. "Come in, Mr. Jared."

Jared dismounted and followed Kate into the kitchen. He saw Nona and Otis Newman sitting at the kitchen table facing each other.

"We were just talking about you, Mr. Jared."

"I guess that's why my ears were burnin'," Jared said, smiling. "Is Frank Dunn around, ma'am?"

"He left this morning, Mr. Jared," Kate said. "He went out looking for our cattle."

Jared nodded. Kate told him to sit while she poured him a cup of coffee.

"Thank you, ma'am," Jared said. He took a sip and smiled at the young lawyer. "Nice job you did on the Judge, Mr. Newman."

"You did well yourself, Mr. Jared. Your testimony was what won over the jurors."

"I'm sorry you and your daughter had to suffer it, Mrs. Beckett," the cowboy said. "I truly am sorry."

"I'm not," Kate said. "I'm glad it was all hung out for the valley to hear. They needed to know."

"I assure you, ma'am, I meant no disrespect."

"I believe you, sir," Kate replied. "What brings you this far from the Circle V, Mr. Jared?" Kate asked.

"Well, I'm no longer with the Circle V, ma'am. You couldn't use an extra hand, could you?"

Kate chuckled. "I could use quite a few hands, Mr. Jared. But right now is a bad time. The bank is going to foreclose on me any day now. Mr. Newman was just explaining my options, such as they are."

The young lawyer cleared his throat.

"I was just saying that Mrs. Beckett would still get some money from the Flying B if she sold it."

"How's that?" the cowboy asked.

"The ranch is worth a lot more than she owes on it, so she would get the balance after the sale. Also, she could stay here until a buyer makes a favorable offer."

"Van Buren will make first offer," Jared said. "He'll bid low and nobody will bid against him. He'll see to that."

"I see," Newman said. "I'm new here, so I didn't know it could get that rough."

"Oh, it can get rougher than that," Jared chuckled. "In fact it can get real bloody."

"I see."

"What if Mrs. Beckett didn't want to sell? She has deep roots in the valley. Her folks were here long before Van Buren showed up with his money," Jared said.

The young lawyer thought about that for a moment and shrugged.

"Then it would be up to the bank to decide what action to take. It could give her an extension or it could evict her by force. Then, as you say, things could get real nasty."

Jared thought for a moment. "I've been through a few of these things. There's one way to stop the bank."

"How is that?" the lawyer asked.

"I could get every small rancher in this valley to side with the Flying B. There's a bunch of them out there who have been in the same situation as Mrs. Beckett is right now. They would fight and bleed for her at the drop of a hat."

"And you?" Kate asked.

"Yes, ma'am. And me."

"This isn't your fight. You could mount up and ride out of here and never look back," Kate said. "You could put all this behind you."

Jared faced Kate. He looked down into her eyes.

"That would be the easy thing to do, ma'am but it wouldn't sit right on my mind in the coming days," Jared said. "I have to set things right."

"Because you killed my husband?"

"That's a big part of it, ma'am, yes."

For a moment they stared into each other's eyes. Here was the man who killed her husband because he'd laid hands on her and now he was willing to die for her. She didn't understand but she wanted him to reach out and take her in his arms and hold her close and tell her everything would be fine. That she would wake up in the morning and all her troubles would be gone.

Nona broke the spell.

"All our cowboys are gone, Mr. Jared," she said. "They've run off or been killed."

"Do you have any proof?" Newman asked.

"No, but they complained about somebody shooting at them out on the range," Kate said.

"I'd say that Van Buren had a hand in that, Momma," Nona said. "Who else would want to do a thing like that?"

"You should see the marshal, Mrs. Beckett," the lawyer said. "Ask for his help."

"Yes I suppose I should," Kate said. "Will you stay for supper, Mr. Jared?"

"I was hoping you'd ask," Jared chuckled.

"And you too, Mr. Newman?"

"Perhaps some other time, Mrs. Beckett, thank you," Newman said. "I'd better be going now. May I call on your daughter in the future ma'am?"

"If she's so inclined, yes, you may," Kate said.

Nona nodded. "I would be honored, sir."

The young lawyer left. Nona started preparing supper. Jared and Kate sat on the porch in rocking chairs watching the sun dip lower in the west behind a stand of silver aspens that shivered in the cold October air.

"You have a nice place here, Mrs. Beckett."

"I'd like you to call me Kate, Mr. Jared."

"I will if you call me Clay."

"Alright, Clay."

Jared looked across at Kate Beckett.

"I'm going to stay in the bunkhouse," he said. "You and the girl are going to need help. Dunn and I will be here until it's over and things are set right. Van Buren wants to destroy you. I won't let that happen."

She reached over and put her hand on his.

"Is that what you want, Clay?"

"Yes," Jared said.

They sat there watching the sun disappear behind the trees. A cold wind scudded up across the yard from the bunkhouse.

11.

While Clay Jared was at the Flying B Ranch, Frank Dunn was walking his horse quietly through a stand of pine trees. Gowdy and his three gunnies, Cord McBride, Windy Johnson, and Nobby Brown, were a quarter of a mile ahead. Dunn could see them and they seemed to be heading west. Suddenly they rode over a rise and he lost sight of them.

Dunn stopped when he came to the far side of the trees. He saw a large, open field and the tall broomsedge showed clearly where the horsemen had cut across, trampling it down. The cowboy walked his horse in the same direction.

The trail led another three miles through cottonwood and birch and finally came out into a large, low, flat area. Even before he got there Dunn heard the sound of cattle. He stopped at the very edge and looked down at a large herd. There was no one in sight.

Dunn dismounted and tied his horse to a sapling. He got some jerky and hard tack from his saddlebag, and took his canteen over to a clump of bushes and sat down to eat and watch. The sun was low in the west, just above the top of the pines on the far side of the field.

After about twenty minutes nothing happened so he mounted up and walked his horse slowly down to the herd so as not to spook it. He checked and found the brands were those of the Flying B.

But they were on Circle V land!

As he sat there pondering the situation he heard the sound of hoof beats to his rear. Just as he turned to look, a bullet whipped past close to his head, followed by the sound of a rifle blast. Two more shots followed that. Dunn turned his horse and got it moving across the back trail in the direction of the Flying B.

In that quick backward glance, he recognized Gowdy, McBride, Johnson and Brown.

The Circle V men were coming on fast and Dunn dug his heels in to get his mount moving faster. It responded with a sudden burst of speed and sprinted into the trees. Once in there it was a game of dodge, swerving left and right to avoid smashing into the trunks and branches. The young cowboy leaned low over the saddle horn putting slack in the reins and letting the horse have its head.

The Circle V men were getting closer. They spread out in a line and took random snap shots at the fleeing cowboy. A bullet tore through Dunn's hat and one nicked his left boot. Thankfully it was getting darker by the second and they couldn't get a clear bead on him.

Trees sped by him like pickets on a fence. The horse crashed through bushes, terrified as shot after shot rang out and bullets tore splinters from the trees near its head.

Just as he came out of the stand into the open and up a rise, the young cowboy felt a stinging blow in his left side. In a few moments it felt wet and warm. He knew then he was shot. He gritted his teeth, dropped the reins, and held one hand on the wound. He grasped the saddle horn with his free right hand and used his knees to guide his mount.

After a few miles he began to feel the pain. In the darkness he could hear the horses pounding towards him like the hammers of hell.

He wondered if he would make it back to the Flying B.

12.

Jared and Kate Beckett were just about to go back into the kitchen when Dunn came crashing up into the yard. He slid out of the saddle and hung onto the horn with his right hand. They ran down into the yard to him.

"I got winged!" Dunn groaned.

Jared got an arm around the kid's shoulder and helped him into the kitchen where they sat him down in a chair. Nona got the medicine box from the cupboard and handed it to her mother. Kate opened Dunn's shirt to get at the wound.

Nona stared at Dunn. "You ain't gonna croak, are ya, Dunn?"

"It sure feels like it, Miss Nona," the young cowboy said. Then, "Could I have a kiss before I go?"

Nona chuckled. "I guess you ain't hurt so bad."

"It's stopped bleeding," Kate replied as she sloshed some alcohol on a rag and wiped the wound clean.

The cowboy winced and groaned. The bullet had cut a neat ridge in his left side.

"Is it bad?"

"You got tagged good but you'll live," Kate said as she put the medicine box away.

"What happened?" Jared asked.

"I tracked Gowdy and his men to where they got the Flying B cows stashed in a valley on the Circle V," Dunn said. "I saw about a thousand head, but I think there's more in the same area."

"I wonder if Van Buren is aware of it?" Kate asked.

"I suspect he is, ma'am," Jared said.

Nona got some bowls and spoons from the cupboard and went to a big pot of stew on the stove. She filled the bowls and put them on the table.

"You better eat this, cowboy," Nona said to Dunn. "You look about to die of hunger." Dunn dug in.

"Who is this Gowdy?" Kate asked.

"He's been laying low at the Circle V for some time now. I noticed him when I was ramrod there. He was hired before my time by the ramrod I replaced, old Nat Rogers."

"I wonder if he's behind all my missing cowhands?"

"If he is, you can bet Van Buren is too," Jared said. "Maybe I should ask the marshal to check Gowdy out. See if there are any warrants out for him."

"What we should do, pard?" the young cowboy said, "Is take the marshal out to see the stolen cattle."

"Good idea," Jared said. "Will you be able to ride by tomorrow morning?"

"I sure will."

"Alright. We'll see Marshal Talbot in the morning," Jared said. "I'm sure he'll be happy to see me after all the trouble I've caused him."

They all chuckled.

Jared and Dunn slept in the empty bunkhouse that night and after breakfast rode into Saggersville to see the marshal. They told him the story about the stolen herd.

"Alright," the marshal said. He turned to one of his deputies. "You go with them, Owens. Make sure it's like they say."

They rode out and finally got to the place. It had been a long ride and it was well into the afternoon. There was nothing there. The valley was empty.

"You sure this is the place?" Owens asked.

"Sure," the cowboy said. "Just look at the tracks."

"That don't tell us nothin'," the deputy said. "They could have been made by Circle V cattle."

Dunn looked defeated. He stared around. Finally he pointed to a choke point leading out of the valley. It was wide enough to run a herd of cattle through. Jared and the deputy followed the young cowboy over to it. It led into a larger, open range. There were plenty of tracks but no cattle.

"I guess they stampeded them, scattered them all to hell," Dunn sighed. "The smart bastards."

"Sorry, kid," the deputy said.

They turned their horses and rode back towards town.

By the time Jared and Dunn got to the Flying B, it was time for supper.

13.

"Thet was a smart move boss," Cord McBride said to Bart Gowdy. "We scattered that herd all to hell and gone!"

"Yeah," Windy Johnson chuckled. "It'll be a long time before they start drifting back to the Flying B."

Nobby Brown nodded in agreement. Suddenly he grimaced and started fanning the air in front of his face.

"Fer cryin' out loud, Johnson," Brown cried, "You better lay off thet Mex food! Yer stinkin' up the place."

The Circle V bunkhouse was empty except for Gowdy and his companions. The new ramrod had a scheme. He sent all the Circle V cowboys out on the range while he stayed back. An hour latter McBride, Johnson and Brown would drift unseen back to the bunkhouse and play cards with their boss.

"Yeah," McBride said. "Them farts a yers is deadly, Johnson. They're bad enough to make the grass dry up an' die."

They all laughed a moment then settled down.

"You know, boys," Gowdy said. "I'm gettin' mighty tired a ridin' this range. We've been hangin' out fer what, five years now? Maybe it's time ta swing back inta action an' rob a few banks."

"Yeah," Brown said. "Them was the good ol' days, boss."

"But I sure don't want ta ride away empty handed," Gowdy continued. "We should have somethin' ta show fer our hard work, doncha think?"

The others all nodded.

"And maybe raise a little hell on the way out," McBride chuckled.

"Sure boys, we kin do thet, too," Gowdy said.

"What do ya have in mind, boss?" Johnson asked.

Gowdy said, "Fer now, jest keep a doin' what we're doin'. I'll let ya know when it's time ta make a move."

"What about Van Buren?" Johnson asked.

The old outlaw sneered. "Him and thet stuck-up wife of his stick in my craw. No wonder they ain't got no kids. She couldn't stand the bother of it."

"Well, he sure knows how ta get around her. He spends more time in town than he does in her bed," McBride chuckled.

"Yeah," Johnson sneered. "An' he's got somethin' on the side over at the Regal Hotel."

"He does?" Gowdy asked.

"Oh, yeah," Johnson said. "I talked ta her. She's a sweet little thang, she is. She use ta be a regular over at the Dirty Boot Saloon before Van Buren picked her up."

They all laughed then fell quiet. A chilly wind rattled the windows. Chickens cackled out in the yard. Finally McBride spoke.

"I wonder what he keeps in thet big safe in his study?"

"Yeah. Thet's what I've been a wonderin', too," Brown mused.

"Wal, before we ride outta here I'd sure like ta find out," Johnson said.

"Hell," Gowdy said, "maybe we will, boys. Maybe we will."

Later that evening, after dark, Van Buren sent for Bart Gowdy.

"Ya wanted ta see me, boss?"

Van Buren smiled. He seemed unusually friendly.

"Yes, Gowdy," Van Buren said. "Have a seat."

The old outlaw took a chair facing Van Buren. The rancher opened the cigar box on the desk, took one, and offered one to Gowdy. The old outlaw was surprised but he quickly took it and they both lit up. In moments a cloud of gray smoke swirled above their heads.

"What kin I do fer ya, boss?"

"How's it going with the Flying B?"

"Pretty good, boss. Especially with their cows. I've got 'em whittled down to about six hundred head now, an' all their cowhands are gone."

"Oh? What happened to them?"

The old rustler wasn't that stupid. Van Buren wanted incriminating details and Gowdy knew it. He chuckled. "Hell, I guess they got scared and ran off, boss."

Van Buren chuckled. "Sure they did." He knew Gowdy killed at least some of them, and he knew he'd never say it outright.

"Is thet all, boss?"

Van Buren gave Gowdy an intense stare.

"No, no!" He turned his chair around to face the big safe behind him. He spun the dial to open it. Reaching in, the rancher took out a small pile of bank notes and placed it on the desk. The outlaw stared at it.

"What's thet, boss?"

"Five hundred," Van Buren said. "It's yours if you make one thing happen."

"What's thet, boss?"

"You make somebody disappear like you did the Flying B cowhands and it's all yours, Gowdy."

"You mean her?" Gowdy asked. Van Buren nodded.

The sly old rustler pretended to balk. "I don't know, boss. Killin' women, thet's serious. I'd be breakin' the code. They hang ya fer that."

"A thousand, then."

"A thousand?"

"Half now and half after it's done."

Gowdy held off for a moment.

"Okay," he said. "It's a deal boss."

Later, as Gowdy walked back to the bunkhouse with five one-hundred-dollar bank notes in his pocket, he smiled. He saw the pile of bank notes in the safe. They must be worth thousands and all for the taking. If he was bold enough and smart enough he could ride out on his own with the whole bundle.

Robbing banks and stealing cattle was hard work best done by men younger than he was. You dodge posse after posse for the rest of your life, and selling branded cattle was hard work in itself. And now even the small-town banks were on their guard.

By the time Gowdy got back to the boys, he had a plan in mind. It was Friday night and most of the Circle V boys were already in town getting drunk. He took McBride, Johnson and Brown aside.

"Why don't you boys go on into town ta get drunk an' raise hell like the rest?"

"Ain't you a comin', boss?"

"Sure, but Van Buren wants me ta take care of something fer him, first. I'll be along as soon as I get it done." He dug two double eagles out of his pocket and gave them to Brown. "Git an extra bottle of whiskey fer me."

They nodded and went out to saddle up and ride for town.

Gowdy waited until they were gone and mounted up. He rode west across Circle V land in the darkness. In two hours he was at the Flying B ranch house, stopping his horse down by the fence. He saw lights in the kitchen window.

"Hey, in the house!" he yelled. "It's me, Bart Gowdy!"

A few moments later Jared and the kid came out on the porch. Kate followed. There was enough moonlight for Gowdy to see she carried a shotgun.

"Whatta ya want, Gowdy?" Dunn hollered back.

"I see ya made it kid. McBride figured he'd a drilled ya good."

"Nope, he jest winged me a little is all."

"Yeah, well, he sent me out ta tell ya he'll be a waitin' at the Dirty Boot Saloon with Brown and Johnson. They want a square shot at you and Jared."

"They do, huh?" Jared replied.

"Yep. Unless you an' the kid ain't got the grit ta face 'em!" Gowdy chuckled loudly. "What's it gonna be?"

"Tell 'em we're on our way, asshole," the young cowboy said. "You gonna be there, too?"

"Who, me?" Gowdy laughed. "Hell, don't worry about me, kid. If you git past my boys, I'll be lookin' fer you myself. You kin bet on thet, buckaroo."

"Good enough," Dunn said.

"Oh, Jared," the old outlaw yelled, "you kin have yer job back. Ramroddin' the Circle V ain't sech a hot job after all."

With that, Gowdy kicked his horse and rode off.

Jared turned to Dunn. "I guess we've been braced, kid."

"Looks like it."

"Don't go," Kate said. "It's a trick."

"You think so, ma'am?" Dunn asked.

"Yes."

The young cowboy shrugged. "I gotta go anyway, ma'am. If I don't, I won't be able to show my face in town. I'd be branded as a coward. I couldn't live with that. They'd call me a coward everywhere I went."

"He's right," Jared said. "It goes for me, too. A thing like that follows you around."

There was an awkward moment of silence. A coyote howled back in the pines. The kid sighed.

"In case I don't come back, give Miss Nona my regards, ma'am."

Before she could answer, Frank Dunn walked down the porch steps toward the stable. Kate put a hand on Jared's arm.

"Be careful," she said. He nodded and left.

In half an hour the kid and Jared rode out for town.

For a while no one spoke. Then Dunn said, "I think it was Gowdy who had Brown steal your watch, wasn't it?"

"Yes. But it doesn't matter."

"Why not?"

"Because he'll be dead in an hour."

14.

A cold October night wind blew at their backs as Dunn and Jared followed the road to town past waving fields of prairie grass and swaying aspens whose leaves rang like a thousand harps as the invisible fingers of nature stroked them.

The moon that night had the same October hue of the Hunter's Moon of old. It looked like a huge copper ball suspended by invisible ropes above the town of Saggersville. Part of it was missing as if an angry beast had bitten a chunk out of it, leaving three-quarters of it to gloat down at the town.

As they came cautiously and slowly along the road, Jared looked at his young companion. "You ever did this before, kid? Besides shoot holes in a tin can?"

"No. You?" The kid was a bit unsure of himself.

"Yeah."

"A lot?"

"Yeah."

"Any advice?"

"Yeah. Watch their eyes. They'll blink just before they draw. We all do it. It just happens." Jared paused to think. "Keep yer legs spread a little an' face them square on. As you draw, swing yer hips. Keep yer gun hand in line with yer right leg, bein' as yer right handed."

"What if they don't blink?"

"They will, unless they're professionals."

"If they are?"

"Then we're both in the crapper, kid," Jared chuckled. Then, in a serious voice, "And don't stand close to me. Stay at least ten feet away. That's important."

The kid nodded.

The moon was behind the town when they rode into Saggersville and tied their horses to the rail in front of the mercantile store. They checked their Colts to make sure they had a full cylinder. Dunn looked at Jared with an uncertain look on his face.

"Scared, kid?"

"Yeah. Real scared."

"That's good. Stay scared."

They walked a few yards then stopped. Jared turned to the young cowboy and put a reassuring hand on his shoulder.

"I shot my first man when I was seventeen, kid. I caught him red-handed stealing my horse and rig. I was scared and didn't know what to do. He had a gun and I braced him. I didn't even remember drawing but when it was over he lay dead on the ground and I'd pissed my pants."

Dunn chuckled. "Thanks but the last part was a little more than I needed to know, pard."

"You'll do just fine, my friend."

They walked slowly up the street towards the Dirty Boot Saloon, meeting very few people on the way. A cat ran across Dunn's path and almost got tangled in his feet. The cowboy cursed then laughed nervously. A dog barked down an alley.

"What about the marshal?" the kid asked.

"What about him?" Jared said.

"Shouldn't we tell him?"

"He'll know soon enough. Besides, if we tell him, he might decide ta lock us up."

"Yeah. He probably would." He chucked again. "A nice cozy jail cell would feel pretty good right about now."

They finally stood on the porch of the Dirty Boot Saloon staring at the batwing doors. The oil lamps inside cast a pale, bluish light outside. A drunk came staggering through the doors and down the steps. He tripped, fell to his knees, cursed, got back up, and stumbled away into the dark.

Jared and Dunn both took a deep breath and exhaled.

"You ready for this, kid?" Jared asked.

"Hell, why not? Let's get this dance started."

Jared nodded and they went quickly into the Dirty Boot Saloon.

The barroom was dark and shadowy. Cigarette and cigar smoke swirled and danced above in the dull light of the sputtering oil lamps that hung from the rafters. Cowboys, town folk, tradesmen and women jammed the place full. Some of the women were girlfriends and some were on the prowl. The stench of stale tobacco rose up from the overflowing spittoons on the floor by the bar.

Somewhere in the back someone plunked away at Camptown Races on an out-of-tune piano. Every few bars the player hit a key that had a weird sound and threw him off stride. He would start all over again from the beginning.

Jared and the kid stopped about ten feet in front of the swinging doors and spread out, the kid to the right and Jared to the left. He took up the stance, and the kid did, too.

They stood waiting. In a few seconds people started to take notice and began to whisper knowingly. A shootout was in the making. Whispers went around the room fast as a lightning strike. People at the bar and tables began to move over by the far wall creating a large open space all the way to the back room.

The piano playing suddenly broke off. It was quiet enough to hear someone sneeze back in the shadows.

McBride, Johnson, Brown and another man dressed in the black of a gunslinger stepped out into the open space thirty feet away, facing the kid and Jared. They took up the stance, too.

A bent-over old man came out of the crowd and limped down the middle of the room past Jared and Dunn. He went out the batwing doors complaining and mumbling.

"Whose yer fancy dressed pal, McBride?" Jared said asked.

"Phil Tanner," McBride said. "Maybe you've heard of him. The Red River Kid?"

Jared chuckled. "He's called a kid, is he? Hell, he looks old enough to be my grand pappy!"

A few nervous chuckles came from the crowd of watchers.

Suddenly the bartender pulled a scattergun from beneath the bar.

"Take it outside, boys!"

The new guy, Tanner, drew with lightning speed and shot the bartender. The bullet smashed into his shoulder and he accidently pulled the trigger of the scattergun. It boomed loudly and sprayed buckshot into the wall above the crowd.

That started the dance.

Jared drew and fired from a crouch, hitting Tanner in the chest knocking him spinning backwards. The gunny bounced off a table and hit the floor face down. McBride snapped off a hasty shot at the kid, missing the kid's head by an inch, taking the hat off his head. The kid answered with a clean shot to McBride's belly. Johnson also got off a shot at the kid, nicking him in his left arm. Jared turned to Johnson and shot at an angle, hitting him between the eyes, dropping him like a rock. Brown was just about to put a bullet into Jared when the kid spun to the left and drilled him in the chest. The shot slapped Brown flat on his back. As he fell he fired his Colt up into the air and narrowly missed an oil lamp.

It was all very quick and loud and filled the air with the smell of gunpowder. Both Jared and the kid stood frozen in place, their eyes searching the room. Nothing moved. They stood erect and looked at each other. They nodded and holstered their guns. The kid got his hat and they walked slowly out of the Dirty Boot Saloon into the night.

Halfway back to their horses they met the marshal and his deputies. They were excited.

"What the hell was all thet shootin' about, Jared?"

"Hell if I know, marshal," Jared said.

The marshal and the deputies rushed up the road towards the Dirty Boot Saloon. Jared and Dunn stood watching until they went in then walked on chuckling.

When they came to the mercantile they stopped a moment to get settled. The kid was shaking badly. Suddenly he ran behind the building and threw up. When he came back he looked unsettled and pale.

"That's how it gets you the first time, kid," Jared said. "You okay? How's yer arm? Can you ride?"

"I'm okay, I guess. Just sick in the gut is all," Dunn said.

"Well, yer a pro now," Jared said. "And I'm damn proud to call you a friend and partner."

They shook hands, mounted up, and rode for the Flying B Ranch. The moon was gone now and it was pitch black except for a strange afterglow. They could just see the road that stretched like a faint silver ribbon to the west before them.

"I wonder why Gowdy never showed up?" the kid asked.

"Good question, kid."

After that, they didn't talk.

15.

After leaving the Flying B Ranch, Bart Gowdy rode back to the Circle V as fast as he could. As he galloped along he glanced up at the copper colored moon and thought back to the past.

In his early days, long before he turned to rustling and robbing banks, he was a cowboy. On the long weeks out on cattle drives, the drovers would sit around the campfires at night and tell tall tales.

Gowdy recalled one particular story told about the Comanche Indians. It was said they had a ceremony in October that involved the Hunter's Moon coming out. When the moon was angry, the story went, it showed its anger by turning bloody red. To appease the angry moon god, a young buck would reach his arm into a pit full of copperheads and hold it there until he was bitten. If he lived, that meant he was in harmony with the gods. If he died, it meant he was out of harmony and the gods rebuked him.

Of course young Bart believed every word of it for many years. But not now, not anymore.

As Gowdy rode along he thought about the future, his future. He had plans now and they didn't include McBride, Johnson or Brown. They had served their purpose. Gowdy was going to ride a new trail and they couldn't come with him.

But he had to work fast, hoping that none of his pals would survive the shootout he had set up at the Dirty Boot Saloon in Saggersville.

By the time Gowdy rode into the yard of the Circle V, it was past midnight. The bunkhouse was dark and quiet. Up at the ranch house there was a light on in the study where Van Buren awaited his return. The old outlaw was ready for him.

Gowdy walked silently up the porch steps and looked through the study window. Van Buren was going over some ledgers, figuring out expenses versus profits and so on, as he did every Friday night.

Gowdy tapped on the front door and walked into the hallway.

"That you, Gowdy?" Van Buren called out.

"Yeah, it's me, boss!" Gowdy said as he walked into the study to see Van Buren working by the light of an oil lamp.

"Sit down," the rancher said. He pulled a bottle of brandy and two shot glasses from the bottom drawer of his desk and set them next to the oil lamp. "Well," he finally asked, "did you take care of that little problem of mine?"

"I did it, boss, jest like I said I would."

Van Buren smiled and leaned forward in his chair with his elbows on the desk. He stared at Gowdy.

"Sit down."

Gowdy pulled a chair up close to the desk and plopped down in it. He was exhausted from the long ride.

"You looked bushed," the rancher said. He poured two shot glasses full of brandy and handed one to the ramrod. "Here's to the Circle V. May it grow and grow."

Van Buren sipped his drink. The old outlaw knocked his down in one gulp and wiped his stubbly chin. He licked the inside of the glass then put it back on the table.

"Good rotgut, boss," Gowdy chuckled. "Damn good." Then he said, "How's about one of them fancy cigars of yours?"

"Of course!"

The rancher took a cigar from the cigar box and handed it to Gowdy. The outlaw put it in his mouth and lit it.

"Tell me all about it, Gowdy," the rancher said. He took out another cigar for himself. In a moment there was a cloud of smoke vapors circling around the oil lamp.

"Well," Gowdy started out, "McBride, Johnson, Brown an' me, we got out there jest as dark set in. We tied our broncs back in the woods jest ta be sure nobody would hear us, then snuck down to the ranch house unseen. The bunk house was empty 'cause we'd already killed all her cowhands. Them as we didn't git ta kill, well, they run off."

Gowdy took the cigar from his mouth and stared at the embers on the end of it.

"Hell, those thet got away are probably still runnin' scared," Gowdy said and chuckled.

"Go on. Did you?" Van Buren was hungry for the gory details.

"Oh, sure. We jest snuck up on the porch quiet as injins. But that kid, Dunn, and Jared mustta heard us 'cause they came out."

"Dunn and Jared were there?"

"Yep and they walked right into our guns. We shot 'em both all to ribbons boss. They didn't have a chance."

Having said that, Gowdy chuckled and knocked cigar ashes off on the rug. Van Buren didn't like that but said nothing.

"Go on! Then what happened?"

"Well, we ran into the house and cornered thet snooty young lawyer, the woman, and the girl in the kitchen. She made a move fer a scattergun but I grabbed her by her scrawny throat. She kicked and hollered but I twisted it like she was a chicken an' her neck snapped like a twig."

The old outlaw paused to take a puff on his cigar. The rancher couldn't wait to hear more.

"Go on!" he said eagerly.

"Well, McBride grabbed the girl and took out his skinnin' knife and cut her head half off. Christ, boss, you shoulda seen it! There was blood a spurtin' all over the place. Johnson shot the lawyer four times in the head. His brains splattered on the stove and caught fire. What a stink thet made! You shoulda been there, boss."

Van Buren looked a bit uncertain. The story had shaken him up by its sheer gruesomeness. He forced a smile. Gowdy saw the rancher's discomfort and was pleased.

"Good job," the rancher heard himself saying.

He turned his chair towards the safe. He wanted to get Gowdy out of his house as soon as possible. Had his wife been listening? She was a sneak and a snoop. He shivered a moment as he opened the safe and took out a large stack of bank notes.

He started peeling some off onto the desk.

"Don't bother, countin', boss," Gowdy said. "I'll jest take it all, if ya don't mind."

For a moment Van Buren kept on counting but suddenly realized what the man had said and stopped.

"What?"

"I said, don't bother counting it out, boss. I'll jest take the whole thing."

Van Buren's eyes narrowed.

"Is that a joke, Gowdy?"

"It's no joke, boss."

"And if I object?"

Gowdy smiled. "Then I'll have ta kill ya, boss."

Van Buren dropped the stack of bank notes and reached into his desk for a gun. Gowdy quickly pulled his boot knife and lunged forward, driving the blade into the ranchers' heart. For a moment Van Buren stared blankly at the outlaw then slowly sat down. A gurgling sound bubbled up from his mouth as he slumped back in the chair with the handle of the knife sticking out of his chest.

Gowdy pulled the blade out, cleaned it on Van Buren's shirt, and then put the knife back in his boot. He began gathering up handfuls of bank notes and stuffing them into his pockets. When he had them all, he turned to leave.

It was then he saw the hulking figure of Thelma Van Buren standing in the doorway in her night robe, pointing a double-barreled shot gun at his chest."

"Mrs. Van Buren!" Gowdy said in surprise.

"Mr. Gowdy!" Mrs. Van Buren growled.

The old ramrod reached for his Colt and he and Mrs. Van Buren fired at the same time.

The blast from the scattergun smacked the outlaw in the chest and slapped him backwards over the desk like he'd been hit with a sledgehammer. He landed with the soles of his boots sticking up over the edge of the desk. His heels did a quivery little dance then stopped as he died.

Mrs. Van Buren dropped the shotgun and walked slowly over to a chair and sat down. Gasping for air and looking very pale, the big woman glanced down to where Gowdy's bullet had entered her chest. She shuddered, slumped over sideways, tilted her chin down, and closed her eyes with a sigh.

In the morning the woman who did the house cleaning came and found the three bodies.

16

After a year, the Circle V Ranch was placed on the county tax rolls as property up for sale. The Van Burens had no surviving kinfolk and there was no one who could make a claim or had a lien on their property. So the Circle V was broken off into three smaller ranches and the thirty or so cowboys found work on them or elsewhere in the valley.

Clay Jared and the kid spoke to a bunch of them in the Circle V bunkhouse before they left.

"Men, you know me. I was your ramrod for a piece. I never lied or cheated on you," Jared said. "I'm asking for a favor. The Flying B has fallen on hard times. All its cattle have been stolen and its cowhands dead or gone. It needs help."

Jared knew what was coming next.

"How's she gonna pay us?" someone asked.

"Right now, she can't pay the kid or me. But after the spring drive you'll get all your back wages."

Another cowboy named Martins laughed.

"What's so funny, Martins?" Jared asked.

"Hell, she ain't got no money or no cows. The way I see it, she ain't got shit!"

Jared looked down at the ground for a moment. He was cornered. All he could do was shrug.

Suddenly the kid spoke up.

"She got plenty of cattle," he said.

More chuckles rippled through the crowd.

"Yeah? Well, where the hell are they, asshole?"

"If Gowdy, McBride, Johnson an' Brown were here, they'd sure tell ya," the young cowboy said. "They rustled them all off someplace an' kilt the Flyin' B's cowboys."

Everything went quiet. Finally someone yelled out.

"Whatta ya want from us, kid?"

"I want a dozen a you to come over to the Flyin' B and work for the brand. Gowdy and his men destroyed it and I want ta build it up agin. Thet's all I want from you dumb sons a bitches! An' if any of you assholes wanna go outside and brace me, let's go!"

No one moved or said a word.

"Look," Jared said, "the Flying B cattle are out there someplace. If we kin find them that'll solve the problem. The Flying B will be back in business agin just like it was."

Murmurs ran through the crowd. Heads shook.

"I ain't gonna bust my ass fer free." The cowboy called Martins said. "No way."

Suddenly a voice came from the doorway.

"You'll get paid, cowboy."

Everyone looked toward the door as Otis Newman came into the bunkhouse. Most of the cowboys knew him from the trial in town. He was well liked.

"Who says so?" Martins asked.

"I do," the lawyer said. "I give you my word."

"You own the Flyin' B, mister?" someone asked.

"No, but I represent Mrs. Beckett."

There was further murmuring. Finally someone shouted out, "Hell, I'll take the bookworm's word for it. I'll do it."

"Yeah," another said. "Hell, why not. At least Mrs. Beckett knows how to make a great strawberry rhubarb pie. An' that counts, in my book."

Fifteen cowboys came out of the crowd and gathered around the doorway. They all shook Otis Newman's hand to seal the deal.

"Git goin'," the kid said. "I'll be right behind ya."

Martins led the group outside to saddle up.

"Thanks, Newman," Jared said to the young lawyer. "That's the second time you jumped in to help me."

"My pleasure."

After Newman rode away in his buckboard, Dunn chuckled.

"What's so funny, kid?" Jared asked.

"Hell, he's a doin' it fer Nona. He's in love with her."

"Can you blame him, kid?"

"Hell no!"

Jared and the young cowboy watched as all the remaining Circle V men left the bunkhouse to saddle up and ride out to look for a job. Some would look elsewhere in the valley and some would ride on to new adventures.

Jared and Dunn stood looking around at the empty room. Jared smiled and chuckled.

"Two hard years all gone now, kid."

The young cowboy nodded. "Yeah. Somehow I'm gonna miss this place. And ol' Van Buren, too, in a way."

"Remember O'Leary, the Irishman who used to sing the cattle to sleep at night?"

"Yeah," Jared chuckled. "This place is full of memories, kid. Full of 'em."

"I'm glad we ventilated Windy Johnson. He use ta stink the whole place up after he ate that Mex food."

For a moment sadness seemed to settle in.

"Come on kid," Jared said. "Let's get the hell away from here."

They left.

17.

In early November, after a tireless search of the area, some of the new Flying B cowboys came upon a lone cow near the mouth of a far valley on the furthermost edge of what was once the old Circle V Ranch. The brand was clear. It was a Flying B cow. They rode further in and saw a large herd. There were beeves as far as the eye could see.

It took a whole week to get them all back on Flying B land where the grass was tall and green. By February and March, the two and three-year-olds had dropped their calves. In April the branding began and was over by late May.

That summer, the Flying B had its best trail drive to market ever.

During that time, the young lawyer, Newman, was able to forestall foreclosure by the bank. He also proposed to Nona Beckett. They were married in June and the lawyer moved into the Flying B right after they came back from their honeymoon in California. He rode his buckboard each day to town to conduct his lawyer business.

Soon after that, Clay Jared packed up his gear. He went to see Kate Beckett. She was hanging out clothes behind the ranch house.

"Mr. Jared," Kate said.

"Mrs. Beckett," Jared said.

"Getting restless, are you, sir?"

"Yes, ma'am. A little."

She turned to face Jared.

"You may kiss me once before you go, if you want to, Mr. Jared."

Kate Beckett closed her eyes and tilted her head to one side a little. Jared kissed her once. He went back for a second kiss but she pushed him away, laughing.

"I said once, Mr. Jared."

The cowboy chuckled.

"Maybe I should stay after all."

"No, Mr. Jared," she said. "You'd be happy for a while but then the urge to ride on would hit you. You like danger. It's in your blood, sir."

Jared nodded. "Yeah. I suppose so."

"What about Mr. Dunn?" Kate asked.

"He's yer ramrod, ma'am. You'll get no better man to ride for the brand. Treat him well. He needs to grow roots."

"Aren't you going to say goodbye to him?"

"I don't know how."

Kate nodded. She understood.

"When he comes in I'll say the words for you, if you'd like?"

"I would appreciate that, ma'am."

Jared looked out across the field to where white clouds were piled high on the horizon. An eagle moved effortlessly across the sky. Finally he turned back to Kate.

"Well, ma'am," Jared said, "it's sure been a privilege to have known you."

"And to have known you too, cowboy."

Jared looked away for a moment.

"Well, I guess this is goodbye then?"

"Yes. Goodbye then." Kate's voice was but a whisper. She also looked up at the sky and saw the eagle. When she turned back Jared was walking away.

She watched the cowboy go down to where his horse was waiting by the corral fence. He mounted up and walked the animal past the empty bunkhouse and out onto the road. He stopped once, turned to wave at her, and then rode quickly away. Soon he was out of sight.

Kate stayed there crying for a while then wiped her eyes and finished hanging up the clothes. She looked up at the sky but the eagle was gone.

She picked up the clothesbasket, walked back to the ranch house, and went into the kitchen.

18.

The day was beautiful and Clay Jared rode west, putting the Flying B Ranch far behind him. Puffy white clouds mounted the sky right down to the far horizon. He noticed birds moving across it high above, free to go wherever they wanted to go. He, however, was headed for the Caldwell area. Ranches were hiring near there.

He was soon in the backlands and heading across a wide area of prairie grass where cows stood eating with bowed heads. Beyond that were stands of pine and sloping hills. He passed through some ranchland where cowboys took notice of him. He waved and rode on.

He was a day out when he stopped to make camp in a stand of birch trees near a fast running stream. After slinging his saddle, saddlebags and canteen, he rolled out the blanket using the saddle as a pillow. He cleared a spot for a fire and went to gather up some wood and tinder. The light was fading fast and he wanted to settle for the day.

That's when it happened.

Just as he reached into a pile of dry twigs, he felt something hit the inside of his left palm, down near the wrist where the fleshy part is. It felt like the sting of a wasp. Jared pulled quickly back and saw a copperhead darting into the bushes.

He looked at his hand where he had been bitten. There were two teeth marks just at the edge of the lower palm.

Walking quickly back to camp he lay on the blanket with his head on the saddle, trying to stay calm. His mind raced, trying to recall if copperheads were deadly or not. There were lots of stories, some made up, some true. It was hard to sort the good from the bad.

A minute or two after the bite he started having trouble focusing his eyes. The light seemed brighter and it hurt his head. The birch trees suddenly began to grow twins and the twins also grew twins. They began to multiply at a dizzying rate.

Suddenly he had trouble breathing. It was as if he had swallowed a ball of cotton. He felt very hot and should have been sweating but he couldn't. Such a great weakness swept over him that it took all the strength he could muster to roll on his side and reach for the canteen.

His hand groped aimlessly around but couldn't find it. It felt as if someone had built a fire inside his head and his brain was burning up.

Then the hallucinations came.

First there was his father coming to drag him down to the recruitment center, then came his uncle Remmy with his warm smile. He saw the copperhead moon and Arny Beckett. He shot Beckett again, one more time.

After a while a shadow came and stood over him. It forced water into his mouth and poured it over his feverish head. He began to drift away from the blazing light into a calmer place of peace and quiet.

Finally he slept until the smell of hot coffee and bacon woke him up.

"Howdy, pard!" Frank Dunn said, chuckling. "Welcome back."

Jared tried to sit up. It took an effort but he finally made it. He rubbed his eyes. He was still a little dizzy.

"How long you been here, kid?"

"Two days. You had me guessin' for a while."

"I'm lucky you came along, kid. How come?"

The kid looked at him. "You left without saying goodbye."

'Yeah," Jared said solemnly. "I don't do goodbyes so good. I never could. They're too sad."

"Yeah. I just found that out," Dunn said. "Hell, anyway I just wanted to track you down to say I'm heading back to Chicago."

"Did something happen back there, kid?"

The young cowboy shrugged. "Yeah. Sorta."

"You couldn't get her outta your head, huh?"

"Hell, I knew it would never work out anyway. Her married to the lawyer and me seeing them together every day, all lovey-dovey."

"She really got to you, didn't she?"

Frank Dunn nodded and looked away.

"Well, you got one thing on them, kid."

"Yeah, what's that?"

"You're free as a bird and she and he ain't. They're locked together come hell or high water now, kid."

"I suppose so."

"You know what we both need, kid?"

"No, what?"

"We need to go into Ellsworth and kick up our heels. We need to get all pissy faced drunk and kiss a pretty girl. Maybe five pretty girls. Would you like to do that before you go home?"

The young man chuckled. "Yeah! I'd like to do that, pard, I really would."

"Then that's what we're gonna do as soon I stop seein' double," Jared chuckled.

Dunn poured a cup of coffee and handed it to Jared. He took a sip. "Damn, this sure tastes good! Gimme a slab of that fatback, too, kid."

Dunn laid a piece of bacon over a biscuit and handed it to Jared. He ate it as if he was starved and washed it down with coffee. He got up on his knees and stood on unsteady legs.

"You'd best give it another day, pard," Dunn warned. "I'd hate ta see you break a leg."

Jared laid back on his saddle and inhaled deeply, filling his lungs with the scent of green growing things. It felt good to be alive.

"She gave me a letter for you, Clay," Dunn said.

He handed Jared a small folded piece of paper. The cowboy opened it. It read:

Mr. Dunn is leaving. I understand why. I hope he finds peace and happiness. He's a good man. I just want to tell you that I appreciate what you did for Nona and me. You will always have a place in my heart. Love, Kate

Jared looked thoughtful for a moment. He refolded the note and put is in his saddlebag. His eyes were moist.

He tried to stand up again. This time he made it.

"Kid, I need a bath," he said.

He walked slowly over to the stream and sat down in it with his clothes on.

The kid laughed.

The End

About the Author

R. Annan is a seasoned and traveled author with many interests. As a career serviceman he served in Korea and Vietnam. He also completed a one-year course at the Defense Language Institute at Monterey, California, and graduated from the University of South Florida with a B.A. in Art and Art History. After taking a two-year course in screenwriting at the Hollywood Scriptwriting Institute, he established The Old Time Radio Club Time Machine as both a scriptwriter and an actor.

A Note from the Author

Thank you for reading my book. If you enjoyed it, would you please consider rating and reviewing it? I'd enjoy your feedback. Thank you!

Look for other books to appear soon.